Coming Round

Antony Lishak
Illustrated by Heloise Wire

To Louise.
From
Antony Lishak

A & C Black · London

The Comets Series

First published 1989 by A & C Black (Publishers) Ltd.,
35 Bedford Row, London WC1R 4JH

Text copyright © 1989 Antony Lishak
Illustrations copyright © 1989 Heloise Wire

A CIP catalogue record for this book is available
from the British library.

ISBN 0-7136-3119-8

Filmset by August Filmsetting, Haydock, St Helens
Printed in Great Britain by Hollen Street Press, Slough, Berks.

The blindfold slips and daylight struggles in.
Dip at the tape; a race you have to win.
Though now you see, not everything is clear.
Resume your sleep, pull back a veil of fear.
Beware! Behind those curtains lies the truth.
Your dreams peel back the mask that hides the proof.
And soon you will arrive home safe and sound.
With body well, but mind still coming round.

The Blindfold Slips

What's happening? I'm lying down but I can't move. Can't see either. And my head! Something is squeezing my head. My eyes won't open.

There's something in my arm and something up my nose. Why is my leg up in the air?

What's going on? Can't see or move ... What's that?

'Okay, young man, just checking the old heart-rate. How are you today? Comfy? Being looked after all right, I hope? Good. Fine. Any progress today nurse?'

Who the hell is he? Why didn't he let me answer? Hold on. Heartrate? Nurse? I'm in a hospital!

'No doctor, nothing yet.'

Progress? What is this ... what the hell has happened to me? Oh, my head!

> So I'm in a hospital. That bleeping noise must be my heart. But I can't remember what happened. I wonder if I'm badly hurt.

'Hello Mrs Foster.'
'Hello nurse.'

> Mum!

'How are you today? I hope you got a good night's sleep.'

'I tried, nurse, I tried. How is he? No better?'

'No worse, Mrs Foster, no worse. Sit down and I'll get you some tea. White with no sugar, isn't it?'

'Thanks.'

> Mum! Mum! I'm all right, honest!

'Here you are, Mrs Foster.'

'Thanks.'

'I know it's difficult, but do try and talk to him. Anything might bring him round, and the sound of your voice could help.'

'Okay... Colin, Colin. It's me, your mum... Colin, can you hear me?'

> Yes, yes. I can! I can! Stop crying, I'm fine.

Why can't I open my eyes? It's like everything has stopped working. A living brain inside a dead body. Oh God, what happened to me?

'Nurse! Something's wrong. That bleep is getting faster. What's going on?'

'It's his heart . . . it's beating faster . . . I think he knows you're here.'

'Colin, can you hear me?'

Yes Mum, yes!

'He can! It's getting faster. Colin it's your mother!'

I can hear you, Mum, now stop crying. Oo, my head!

'What's all this I hear?'

'About an hour ago, doctor. Mrs Foster here, was talking to him and there was a definite quickening of his heartrate.'

'So you're going to join us, young man. Well get a move on, your mother wants to hear your voice!'

'Colin! Colin!'

'Don't be anxious, Mrs Foster, these things take time. We've had one good sign and I'm sure we'll soon have another . . .'

'His eyes . . . they flickered!'

'Are you sure?'

'Yes, yes, I'm sure. I've been sitting here for ages. I know they moved!'

'Colin, are you trying to open your eyes?'

Yes, godammit, yes. But they're stuck, they're stuck!

'See, I told you doctor!'

'Marvellous. Keep talking to him, I'm sure he can hear you.'

'Colin, Colin. Come on, love, open your eyes.'

I'm trying, Mum. Oh, my head!

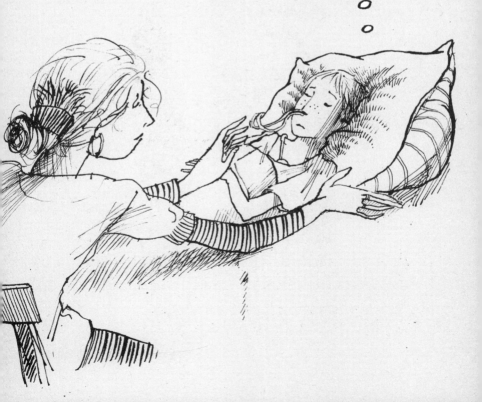

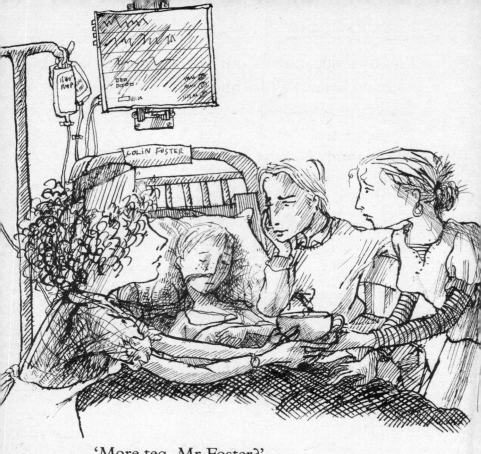

'More tea, Mr Foster?'

'Thanks nurse, yes please. Look, Susan, maybe you were imagining it.'

'But they moved, they moved. Even the doctor saw it.'

'Well he could have just been playing along. You know, so as not to upset you.'

'Don't be stupid, John.'

'Look, it's like when we go fishing. Sitting for hours, waiting for one to bite. Complete stillness for ages, then plop! I'm sure I've got one, pull it in, and nothing. It was all in the mind...'

Shut up Dad, you're spouting rubbish as usual. Mum knows what she's talking about – you don't!

'See, there goes the heartbeat. Nurse! His heart is racing again!'

'Colin are you there, mate?'

Of course I am. Are you blind as well as stupid?

'Come on, love, say hello to your mum and dad.'

'Look, his eyes! You were right, Susan, you were right!'

My head hurts, Mum. It's throbbing all the time. Is Warren with you? Talk to me Mum. Come on, someone say something. Why doesn't it stop throbbing?

My mouth is dry. Tongue stuck to my teeth. Can't even move it. And there's my heart bleeping. Well at least I'm still alive!

Are you there Mum? Dad? Warren? . . . Anyone? No, just the bleep. It's probably night time. They've all gone home.

2

Dip at the Tape

Warmed up now.
When you're ready.
Gently does it.
Keep it steady.
One and two and
Easy breathing
Jog it, run it,
Step it, blow.

Past the garage,
Stretching jogging,
Dodge the dog dirt,
Run it, jog it,
Duck the branches,
Thumping pounding,
Run it, jog it
Half-way done.

Same old lady at the bus stop waiting,
There's that family with the brand new car.
Round the corner is that iron railing,
Last month caught my leg and left a scar.

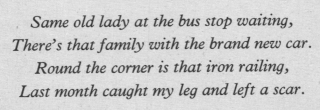

Wish we had a big garden like that one,
Just like playing in a great big park.
Here's that paving stone, loose and wonky,
That's that labrador; hear it bark.

Now the last corner
I've got to make it
And...

Past the bus stop,
You can do it,
Stretch those legs now,
One last go.

Push it
Make it
Come on –
Run it –
You can –
do it –
Almost...
there.

What? Can I see? No, only pictures in my head. Just a dream. But it seems so real.

There's that bleep. Well at least I'm not dead yet. Or could this be what dying actually is, just lying still, hearing and dreaming?

'Well, Colin, your heart's really racing now. You haven't just been for a quick jog up the corridor, heard me coming and popped back into bed, have you?'

Well, actually nurse . . .

There's more noise now, must be morning. I can hear the clanging of the tea-trolley. White, please, four sugars! Wonder when I'll get a visitor.

'Hi brov!'

Warren!

'Look I don't know if you can hear me, but I've got something special here. When the club found out about your accident, Roger did some phoning around and got this message recorded on cassette.'

'Hi Colin, Seb Coe here. Sorry to hear about your little knock. But, knowing you, I'm sure you'll soon be up again and pounding the roads. Take it easy, bye! . . . Hi mate, Daley here. What you doing in bed, squirt? Get up and get some training in! No excuses! See ya' son.'

Fantastic! Brilliant!

'Did you like it, Col?'

You bet. Go on play it again.

'Do you want me to play it again?'

That's what I thought wasn't it?

'Hi Colin, Seb...'

'Any luck, Warren?'

'Not yet, Dad. But I'm sure he can hear it. I get that feeling...'

'I know what you mean.'

I wish I could read a book, or a comic or something. I'm fed up with this blankness. It's like being
in a tunnel that's so long you can't see the end. Keep
seeing pictures. A slow motion film of my life. I saw
Mrs Carter and the rest of the class. They were just
sitting there. Then I saw Mum, Dad and Warren in
the kitchen, just standing like statues. No one does
anything or says anything as if the freeze frame is
on. And when I try to fast-forward it the picture
vanishes and I'm left with a blank screen.

'Hi mate, Daley here . . .'

God knows how many times I've heard that
tape. Warren must be rewinding it. Why doesn't he
speak to me? He used to be my best friend; my big
brother. But lately he's gone all funny. He even
stopped coming training on Mondays. Mum says
he's just growing up and I shouldn't get upset
about it. But I'm growing up too, and I'm not
going all funny. He says he's bored with running
and he's got other things to do. It's not as much fun
since he stopped coming.

'Hi Colin, Seb Coe . . .'

I wonder what happened to me. I've tried to
remember, but the last thing I can think of is
school. I was getting my coat from the cloakroom,
having a chat with some friends and then blank.
Did the school blow up? Did some secondary school
lads beat us up? Or maybe I got knocked down by a
car on the way home. That's impossible, I only

cross one road and there's a lollipop lady and a pelican crossing. You'd have to be a hedgehog to get knocked down there.

'...No excuses! See ya' son.'

'I've had enough of this, I may as well be playing this to a dummy. He can't hear a word of it.'

What the... 'Yes I can you beanhead!'

'Colin!... Nurse!... Colin!... He spoke, nurse, he spoke. I stopped the tape and he told me off!'

'Colin, are you awake?'

That's the nurse's voice. I can feel her breath right next to my face.

'Colin! He's groaning. I can hear it.'

Oh, my head!

'Look, his eyes are opening... He's coming round.'

3

Not Everything is Clear

Running alone tonight
Chase between lampost light
Glide like a bird in flight
Just like a sparring fight.
Racing my shadow.
Duck high then low.

Legs feeling loose and free
Past the old cemetry
And the last chestnut tree
Save up your energy.
Keep that head still.
Now for that hill.

Pound the pavement
You can do it
Never let your shadow win.
Grit your teeth and
Take more air in,
Just ignore that aching shin.

Stomach pain,
Mustn't care,
Push and strain,
Nearly there.
Got to
Make it
Almost . . .
Yes!

It's so bright in here. I'm sure I could open my eyes a little wider if the light was less dazzling. And I'd be able to see my Mum. I can hear her but which one of those ghosts is she?

'Colin, love, it's me. You're going to be fine. The doctor says you're doing well.'

I'm useless. All I can do is moan like a cow. Want to talk. I want to know what happened to me. What if I've lost any parts? And what's wrong with my head?

God I'm stiff! My joints are locked tight and my body's tied down. Tubes up my nose and a needle in my arm. And the pain! What happened to me? I can feel your hands on me and your fingers poking. But why don't you talk to me? Talk to me!

Dark. Quiet and dark. A light breeze tickles the curtains and they sway gently away from the open window. No more bleeps. Funny how you notice things more when they've gone.

I can hear distant footsteps. Hospital footsteps. Hard echoey corridor footsteps. Not coming here. And a snore. Hold on there's another. In a hospital bed you get snores in stereo. A throaty one, just like a pig breathing in, and there's a slobbery one as the pig exhales . . . Welcome to *A night on the farm*, your regular nightly treat to the sounds of animals sleeping. We've already heard from the pig sty and now over to the stables . . . that's the grey, Floppy

Lips. If you get too near her when she sleeps you're likely to get a shower! Well, I'll have to go now, I can hear those footsteps again. This time they're coming closer.

A nurse! After God knows how long, this is the first time I've actually seen a nurse.

'Nurse!' It's not easy to whisper loudly. 'Nurse!'

'Colin? Are you awake? You're a funny lad, four days of sleep then you wake up in the middle of the night!'

'Nurse.' Please sit next to me and let me practise talking again.

'What happened to me?' I'm suddenly scared. I don't know what she is going to tell me. I don't know anything!

'What do you remember?'

My name is Colin Foster. I am eleven years old. I go to Grove Street School and now I'm in hospital and I don't know how, or why, or anything. 'Nothing.'

'You were knocked down. Apparently you were jogging and you ran out in front of a car.'

Impossible. She must have got it wrong. I would never do that. 'I don't remember...'

'Take it easy, there's a good lad, there's no permanent damage. Your leg's broken, you've bruised your ribs and you banged your head. We're in an Intensive Care ward but don't worry, now you've come round the doctors say everything's going to be just fine.'

'Was I being chased?'

'Sorry?'

'Was someone chasing me?'

'Look some people never recall accidents they've been in. Sometimes the memory rubs out things that might be too unpleasant to remember.'

'But someone might have pushed me...'

'The driver would have seen that and she didn't say anything.'

The driver. I never thought of that. There actually is someone who is responsible for all this. Who is she, where is she, why didn't she stop?

'If it's any consolation to you, there were some witnesses who all said that you were sprinting as fast as you could and just ran out on to the road. The driver had no time to see you.'

Sprinting? Now come on, that's definitely wrong. First of all I never sprint while I'm jogging and I'd never sprint out on to a road... 'She's lying!'

'Shush, Colin, you'll wake up the ward.'

'But I never sprint...'

'Look your mind's a little muddled now, and you'll only make it worse by thinking about it. You try and get some rest now and I'll come and see you just before I come off duty.'

I don't believe it. There's two hours of my life hidden away somewhere. I don't understand all this.

23

Maybe that nurse was only another dream. A cruel game that my mixed-up knocked-about brain is playing on me. That must be it. I know I'd never sprint in a jog, and I know I'd always wait and run on the spot at a road if there was a car coming. Yes, another dream, that must be it.

Welcome back to part two of *A night on the farm*. You rejoin us as the night sky gradually gives way to day. The pigs and the horses are silent now. The familiar sounds of morning begin to remind us that a new day is about to start. The rattle of the tea-trolley that brings the precious first slurp of the day to the animals. The rustling of the hay as they wake up, slowly and expectantly. And, of course, the unmistakable sound of the cockerel . . .

'. . . Are you awake, Colin?'

'What? . . .'

'It's me. I said I'd come to see you before I go. How do you feel now?'

Hell, it was no dream! 'Oh, fine.'

'Well I hope you're more cheery than that when your mother comes! Bye!'

4

Veil of Fear

Four days she said. So what day is it today? Well it can't be a Wednesday or Thursday, because the accident happened on a school day. It can't be a Sunday; that man over there is reading The Sun. So it's a Monday, Tuesday, Friday or Saturday. Hold on, it can't be a Monday. Thursday is a swimming day, so I wouldn't have been in the cloakroom at hometime.

Tuesday, Friday or Saturday...Big deal! What difference does it make, I'm not going anywhere.

'Good morning, Colin, I'm Sister McVey. How do you feel?'

'Okay.'

'Good. Now let's tidy up these cards. Dr Bradly is on his rounds.'

Cards? I never noticed them. "Get Well Soon!"

'Who are they from?'

'Well this one says: "Get well bubble-bonce from Spike and Stewart", and this one, "Hurry back to school – Mr Fielding".'

'That's the head!'

'And this one says: "Get well soon from Marcia, Monica, Brian, Andrew...".'

'That's my class!'

'Hello young man, you do look well. Mind if I sit down here?...Let's have a look at this chart then...'

He's just like Fielding! Balding, grey hair. Quite old, fiftyish. Shirt and tie with glasses wedged at the end of his nose. But Fielding doesn't wear a white coat.

'...How's the leg, any pain?'

'No.'

'Good. And the head...comfortable?'

'Yes...'

'Good, good. Now, look straight at the tip of my pen. Follow it, please, as I move it up...down...to the left ... right ... towards you ... and away ... good. Well done. Now, young man, have you any questions you want to ask me?'

Exactly like Fielding. They must be related.
'When can I go home?'

'Oh quite soon. We'll keep a close look on your head for a few days, then if everything's fine we'll have you up on crutches and out of here in no time. I'm afraid the Children's Ward is full right now, but we'll find you a nice place to rest, and get you some books and games and . . .'

'What day is it?'

'Sorry?'

'The day. What day is it today?'

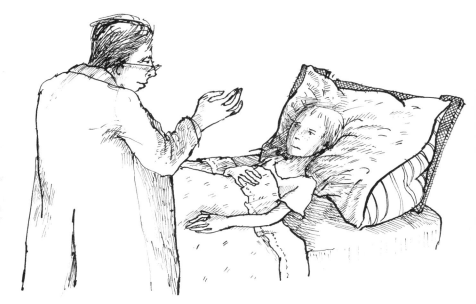

'Friday . . . it's nine o'clock in the morning . . . the sun is shining, birds are singing and all's right with the world. And if your mother plays true to form, she'll be here pretty soon. I'll see you later.'

So it happened on a Monday.

Jog in the rain;
Best time to train.
Vest soaking wet
Rain mixed with sweat.

Skimming the puddles
Dodging the drips,
Rain on my hair
On my eyes, and my lips.

'Colin . . . can you hear me? Colin.'

Bus spits out spray
Socks dirty grey.

'Colin, it's me . . . your mum. Can you hear me?'

'What?'

'He *is* awake! Oh nurse he is . . . look!'

Mum is that you? But I was running. It was raining . . . I just saw this bus . . . it showered me.

'Colin!'

'Sorry about the socks, Mum. I'll wash them myself I promise!'

'I beg your pardon!'

'Mum!'

'What's all that about socks, you silly billy?'

'I was dreaming . . . about jogging . . .'

'Don't you worry your head about that now. You're going to get better first. Forget about your jogging!'

'But I keep dreaming about it. As if I'm really doing it.'

I feel weird. As if I'm not really here. I know that's my mum, but she seems so far off. Like at the end of a tunnel. And the nurse behind her. They look like they're on television.

'He's still half asleep, Mrs Foster. You just sit down. I'll get you a cup of tea.'

Wonder if she knows what really happened to me. But I won't ask; it'll only upset her to talk about it.

'Are you in pain, love?'

'I'm stiff, I wish I could get up. My whole body is stuck in one position.'

'Don't worry, dear. Now they've put you on a proper ward I'm sure you'll be home soon...Everyone sends their love, Dad, Warren, Auntie Edna, Uncle Jack, Grandad...'

'What happened to me, Mum?'

'What?'

Oh, hell, I wasn't going to ask that...it just came out...

'You were knocked over by a car, Colin, while you were jogging. It seems you just ran out in front of it...'

'I didn't. I didn't. It's a lie!'

'Shush, Colin, stop shouting...calm down. Look a nurse is coming now.'

'What's all this noise, then?'

'Leave me alone, you're lying, you're lying...You're all lying!'

'Now stop crying, young man, you're only upsetting your mother. Now what's the matter?'

'It's okay, nurse, he'll be all right now. Won't you Colin?'

No. And it's not okay. You're all lying to me. I'm going to shut my eyes and forget you're there. Then maybe you'll all go away.

'He is still very tired, Mrs Foster. Don't worry yourself about it. It's only normal for him to take a little time to come to terms with it all.'

5

Beware!

'There's a phone call for you, Colin.'

Go away, I'm asleep. I'm not going to open my eyes, now leave me alone.

'Well you must have been awake sometime this morning because your breakfast stuff has been eaten.'

Big deal! Maybe a bird came in through the window and pecked it up! I'm not going to open my eyes, I'm asleep, now go away!

'Well, I suppose I'll have to tell your brother that you don't want to talk to him . . .'

Warren? Why would he phone me? It's only a trick. Very clever, ha ha! Well I'm not going to fall for that one . . .

'Sorry, Warren, but he seems to be asleep still. Maybe he'll ring you when he wakes up. Bye.'

Good, now go away!

'Colin, son. Come on, mate, wake up! It's your dad.'

Of course it's you. Who else would it be? I heard your clomping footsteps half-way down the corridor. If you think I'm going to open my eyes for you, then you're a bigger fool than I thought!

'Look, mate, the doctor says there is no reason why you shouldn't be able to talk. Warren has heard you, that nurse and the doctor spoke with you and you've even been rude to your mother! So come on, Col, stop mucking about and open your eyes.'

Don't call me Col! And there is a reason why I won't talk to anyone. It's because no one will tell me what really happened.

'Okay, young lad, so that's the way you want it. Right, if you don't open your eyes by the time I count to ten I'm going to go.'

Make it three and save your breath.

'Draw the curtains, nurse.'

A new voice. Who's this one, I wonder? Maybe it's the torturer. The one they bring in when the prisoners won't talk. What is it to be, then? Electric shock . . . the thumb screw . . . a tickle under the chin with a feather? Well tough! My lips are sealed and so are my eyes!

'Hello Colin. My name is Doctor Mills. I've come to talk with you. I'd like us to have a chat but if you want to just lie there listening, that's fine by me.'

I'm not listening, so there

'There is something upsetting you, and I'd like you to tell me about it. Will you do that, Colin?'

No.

'We know that you've regained consciousness.

32

And I think you know that we know. And we also know that you aren't sleeping. So there's only one thing left that you could be doing. You're hiding. Hiding from your family and from us. I'd like to find out why, Colin.'

I once stayed like this for hours. Mum thought I was asleep but I wasn't. I sat in a chair and pretended to be dozing because I wanted to see the end of a film on TV. I knew she wouldn't let me stay up otherwise. At least I *heard* the end of the film. I didn't even flicker my eyelids. Afterwards I just stayed in that position, right until she wanted to go to bed. Then she gently shook me. I slowly came around with a dazed look on my face, groaned, stood up, and staggered convincingly to my room. So, Dr Mills, if you think you can get me to open my eyes you've got your work cut out!

'Okay then, I'll have a few guesses. Let's see, maybe you're hiding from having to get up, get better and go back to school. Is that any good?'

Miles off!

'Maybe you don't like your new ward and your hiding from the other patients.'

Still cold, even though they snore ten times louder in here!

'How's about something to do with the lies you said we've told you?'

Very clever, Mrs Interrogator. Start off with a couple of soft ones then come in with the heavy stuff. Well you can't catch me out. I've seen too many of those films!

'Let's see, we said that you were out jogging, when you ran out into the road in front of a car. And you said that we were lying. Is that right?'

You know it is, clever clogs.

'Well, Colin, if we're lying and you know what really happened, don't you think it would be sensible to tell us what you think the truth is? I know that if someone lied to me I'd want to tell them why they were wrong.'

Leave me alone!

'Listen, Colin, whatever is eating away at you inside has got to come out. You're upsetting a lot of people, including yourself!'

She's not going to give up. And I'm going to cry again!

'Come on, Colin, not even you can cry in your sleep and not wake up.'

It's not fair. Why don't you leave me alone? I just want to go home, I don't want to talk to you, I don't want to talk to anyone. Okay, you've made me cry, well done, now go away and leave me alone.

'Look, you will be going home in a few days. Your leg is mending well, your head seems to be fine. We've just got to get you out of bed, loosen you up a bit and off you go. If you don't want to talk then fine. But if you do, then let me know. Okay?

Anyway at least you can eat your lunch now without having to see if anybody's watching you! See you soon then.'

I hope not!

The truth. The truth...How do I know what happened? I was the one who was knocked down, remember? It was my head that was bounced across the road! All I know is that I didn't just run out in front of a car. No way!

And who's this one? Not a nurse, she hasn't got a uniform on. Doesn't look like a doctor either, her coat is different.

'Good afternoon, Colin. I'm a physiotherapist. Do you know what that is?'

'Yes, we've got one at the athletics club.'

'Good. Well I'm going to help you to move about again. Loosen up your arms and your good leg. Are you ready for a bit of work?'

Work? 'What kind of work?'

'Oh, just a few simple exercises to begin with. Nothing an experienced runner like you should find difficult. Right, let's get you sitting up then ...Okay?'

'Yes.'

'Fine. Okay, let's see you try and move those arms then. First the right...slowly now ... good ...can you go any higher? Good. Well done. Now slowly put it back by your side. Any pain?'

'No.'

'Good. Now the same with the other arm. Up...slowly now...good...can you keep it there for just a second? Good...now gradually back down again. Good lad. Now try and bend your good leg. Bring the knee up as gently as you can...good...stop if it's hurting. Fine. Now gradually back down on the bed. Good, how did that feel?'

'Okay.'

'Jolly good. Now I want you to practise those three movements every hour or so. Just do them five times each and stop. When I come back tomorrow you should be ready to get up and try to walk! Bye.'

I feel a right lemon. Up...down...up...down. As if I'm waving to that old guy opposite. And it's making me tired.

Around the corner
Nearly there . . .
But I'm sprinting and I'm rushing
Arms are flaying and I'm screaming
Head is rolling, blindly dashing
Crying, shouting, screaming . . . CAR!

6

The Mask that Hides the Truth

'Colin, your parents will be here soon. I want to tell them that you're a lot calmer now. You know your mother was very upset the last time she was here and your father was none too pleased either!'

So I did run out in front of a car!

'Colin, are you listening to me?'

'Yes.'

'Well? What do you say then?'

'That I was being chased!'

'What?...Are you still worrying about the accident? Look it's not going to help. You should consider yourself lucky that no more damage was done. Now try and settle down and don't upset your parents this time, all right?'

'Okay.'

'Oh Colin, you look fine now, doesn't he John?'

'Good as new!'

They look so worried. I better put their minds at ease.

'I feel a lot better now.'

'Oh, that's so good to hear, dear. Now, everyone sends their love, Auntie Edna, Uncle Jack, Grandad, all your friends ...'

I'll just switch off, and sleep with my eyes open. They'll go on like this for hours...

'... and Margaret next door says hello...'

What made me sprint? Chased by a dog? No, I know all the dogs round there and anyway, a dog would only chase you if you raced away from it. I know that, so I'd have just carried on as usual.

'... went fishing last week, Col, down by the Lea. Didn't have much luck but the weather was superb...'

A person? Why would someone want to chase me? I was wearing my jogging kit so it was obvious I had no money on me. Even if it was someone from Ginger's gang, I'd never run from them, I'm no bottler!

'... we were thinking of doing your room out before you get back. What do you say, wallpaper or paint?'

So if it wasn't an animal and it wasn't a person, what the hell was it? A ghost?

'Well, Colin, what do you think?'

'I don't believe in ghosts, Mum, and I can't think of anything else!'

'What?'

Oh, hell, here we go again...

'You've not been listening to a word we've said! Look, my lad, I've had about as much of your cheek as I can stand...'

'No, John, not now...'

'No, I'm sorry, Susan . . . Your mother wants to molly coddle you, but I'm telling you. If you don't stop feeling sorry for yourself you'll feel the rough end of my tongue!'

'Don't, John, look you've made him cry now.'

'I'm going!'

Good riddance! Oh, but don't you go as well Mum!

I'm scared to sleep. There's no telling what I might see. It's like having a mind like an onion, each dream gradually removing another layer.

The ward is dead now. It's dark outside too. I can hear traffic in the distance. Buses, motorbikes, lorries, the occasional train, cars. Funny how you can recognise different sounds if you try – noisy exhausts, smooth purring engines. Wonder if there's a car with a little dent the size of my leg in the front.

How could that nurse say I was lucky? Some luck! If I'd been lucky there wouldn't have been a car there in the first place. Okay, it could have killed me. But then at least I wouldn't be stuck here wondering what really went on.

And who would miss me anyway? Mum? Well, yes, I suppose so. She'd be really cut up. Dad? No. Oh, he'd be sad at the beginning, but after a month or so he'd say, "Life must go on, there's no use living in the past," and by the end of a year he'd look at my photograph and think, "Things have certainly been quiet round here with you gone." Warren? A couple of years ago he would have missed me. He would have missed playing Three-and-in in the park, helping me paint a model, or our training sessions. But not now. As far as he's concerned I'm just a nuisance. If I died he wouldn't have to put up with me. And at school? Yes, I suppose they'd miss me. There'd be a little mention in assembly. My friends would really miss me, but not for long. Soon I would be the subject that's brought up before every holiday, just to frighten everyone about the dangers of crossing the road. 'Be careful or you'll end up like Colin Foster!'

Well stuff the lot of you! I'm not dead, so you'll just have to put up with me!

I wonder if Warren really phoned? Why should he call me?

Not the best of nights to jog
All is hidden in spooky fog
Can't see very far ahead
Should I stop and walk instead?
Headlights floating calmly by
Streets dead still; But a cry!
Screaming now, just in front of me.
Creeping fog's too dense. Can't see!
'Help! Please stop, please, help me! Stop!'
Bus stop, can't stop, just can't stop . . . !

7

Safe and Sound

'Well that's fine, Colin. I reckon you're ready to try your crutches now.'

Little grey metal things? What a let-down, I wanted old wooden ones. Then I'd only need an eye patch, a stuffed parrot and an old silk scarf, and I'd be just like Long John Silver.

'Okay, now slot your arms in here . . . good, and grip these plastic handles. Now put all your weight on to your good foot. Carefully, now. Right then, just get your balance. Is that comfortable?'

'Yes.'

'Good. Now let's try some small steps. Move your good foot forward . . . put your weight on it, and gradually bring the crutches up level. Good. That's your first step. How's it feel?'

'It's easy . . .'

'. . . Oh, don't be too sure. Just one slip and you could be back in here with your other leg in plaster! You take it nice and slowly to begin with. Now try another step.'

I feel a proper narner! I could hop around faster than this. I'll show her how easy it is . . . 'Ooops!'

'Look out! Be careful, Colin, you nearly slipped then. I told you to take it slowly. I bet you won't do that again in a hurry!'

'You can say that again!'

'Well, are you all ready and packed, then?'

Look who it is! The head torturer, the dreaded Mills! I wondered when she'd be back again.

'You don't look very pleased to be going home!'

Don't look pleased to see you, more like!

'Or do you still blame me for making you cry?'

Look, go away. Just leave me alone...Oh no she's sitting down. I suppose she's going to try to *chat* with me again.

'What's it like to train with Daley Thompson?'

'Sorry?'

'Oh, come on. Ever since your brother brought in that tape the whole hospital's been talking about it. Tell me, is he as good as he looks?'

'What? Daley? He's the greatest. You name it, he can do it. Let me tell you; he is even *better* than he looks!' What an idiot! Who doesn't know that Daley is king?'

'And his fitness. How fit is he?'

This woman is dumb! 'He's super fit. He trains every day, with weights too. He pushes himself all the time. And just before a big competition he builds up to a peak.'

'What do you mean?'

'Well, he carefully plans his training so he can produce a P.B. or better.'

'What's a P.B.?'

'Personal Best, of course!'

'Well, Colin, are you at your P.B. now?'

What does she mean?

'Are you at your peak? I don't mean physically, I mean in your mind?'

Here we go . . .

'I'm sure when Daley goes out into a stadium his mind is free from worries so he can concentrate on athletics. So when you go out this afternoon, will your mind be free from worries?'

Not again!

'Look, Colin. Nothing you say is going to stop you from going home today. I just thought you would like the chance to tell someone what's on your mind. You'll probably never see me again, so it'll make no difference to you. And I promise I'll listen to you, and won't shout you down like your father did.'

'It's the accident.' I can't stop it from coming out now. 'I know I'd never just sprint out into the road for no reason. I was running away from something, but I don't know what it was.'

'Can't you remember anything about that night?'

'I've been having some dreams. I'm always running in them. I even saw the car knocking me down in one. I ran right out in front of it. But the worst one was last night.'

'Why?'

'Well, it was foggy and I was running. I couldn't see a thing, which was stupid because I'd never run in those conditions. Anyway I heard a scream. It was a woman crying for help. Then I woke up all scared and shaky.'

'Do you think it might have something to do with the accident, Colin? . . . Oh, come on, don't cry . . . '

'You're a funny lad!'

What does he want? Why doesn't he stay in his own bed?

'All the time you've been in here, you've hardly spoken to anyone.'

'Well no one exactly made much of an effort to talk to me!' Nosy old goat!

'Oh, you've got a sharp tongue too! Well, maybe it's just as well you kept your mouth shut then!'

Why did they stick me in with a bunch of old men? It's like spending playtime in the staff room with a load of teachers.

'I gather you're going home this afternoon. Bet you can't wait to get out of this place.'

'You can say that again!' Then I won't have to put up with your snoring every night!

'Anyway I just wanted to wish you all the best. And I hope your leg sets as good as new, even though your tongue still needs a bit more time to mend! Oh, and can I ask a small favour?'

Don't tell me, you want Daley's autograph!

'Could I possibly write a good luck message on your plaster cast?'

What? 'Er, yes, why not?'

'Fine. Let's see; "Good Luck, Colin. Keep on jogging, from the old snorer in the bed opposite." There. See you mate!'

'Thanks.' What a sour-head I am. He's quite a

nice bloke, even though I was rude to him. I'm not normally so short-tempered, but I feel so angry these days...

'Goodbye then, Colin, take it easy now, won't you?'

They look like the hospital football team lining up to meet an important person before a Cup Final. I would shake all their hands, but I'd fall off my crutches!

'Come on, Colin. Off we go. Thank you very much for everything, Sister. And, er, this is for you and your staff.'

'Oh, thank you. We'll eat them at tea time.'

'Will you give one to that bloke over there, please, and say it's from me?'

'That's very nice of you, Colin. Of course I will.'

'Bye!'

'You'd better sit in the front, Col, then you'll have room for your leg ... Comfy?'

'Yes.' It's good, this is. I've only ever sat in the front of this car once before and that was because Warren was asleep on the back seat.

'We'll be home in time for tea, love.'

'What have we got, Mum?' I can't wait to get some proper food down me.

'Oh, you just wait and see. I'll let it be a surprise!'

8

Coming Round

Things haven't changed while I've been away. That traffic island hasn't been repaired yet. They haven't even finished cutting down that big tree. Mr Coleman's old Beetle is still decaying in the gutter, but then it's been there for ages. This car hasn't been touched either, there's some pigeon droppings on the front bonnet that splattered on it two weeks ago. And it looks like Warren hasn't repaired his bike yet. There it is in pieces in the front yard. Dad must be livid, I wonder if they're still at each other's throats about it.

'Here we are, home at last.'

The front room curtains are drawn and it's still broad daylight. Something funny is going on here. Mum has just rushed ahead to the house. She's in through the front door before I've even got out of the car!

'Come on, Colin. Be careful up the path, your pain of a brother is slowly turning this place into a scrapyard!'

A dark hallway? Complete silence? Not even the television? I bet I can guess what's about to happen . . .

'Surprise! Surprise!'

What the hell...Auntie Edna, Uncle Jack, Grandpa, Monica, Brian, Alan, Spike, Stewart ...Mr Fielding and Mrs Carter!

'Watcha Bubble Bonce!' – 'Hello Hop-Along!' 'Welcome back, young lad!'

Talk about *This Is Your Life*!

'Hey, let's sign your plaster!'

'Let him sit down, come on. He's just spent a week on his back so let him settle down.'

'You look very well, my boy.'

'Wouldn't you if you'd been in bed for so long?'

'How does it feel to be home?'

'Great!' I must ask it ... I'm dying to ask it ... I'm going to ask it ... 'Sir. Do you have any relatives who are doctors?'

'Not that I know of. Why do you ask?'

'Oh nothing, Sir. I was only wondering.'

'Come on, Brian, get out your felt tip.'

'Keep it clean boys, won't you? He's still got to walk around the school, remember!'

'Yes Miss.'

'Oh, stop stop ... it tickles!'

'Okay, everyone, finish off your cakes. I think that's enough excitement for one day!'

'Very wise, Mrs Foster. Well, it's good to see you fit and about again, young man. I'll look forward to hearing your crutches around the school!'

'See you soon, Bubbles.' – 'Bye!' – 'Take it easy, see ya!'

'We're off too, Colin. We'll come round tomorrow!'

'Bye Grandpa!'

Mum asleep in front of the telly and Dad asleep with the newspaper over his chest. It's as though I was never away. And I bet if I try to change the channel they'll notice and wake up ...

'Hey ... I was watching that!'

'Oh yes, and what was it about then?'

'He's been back a few hours and he's already giving me lip! You just watch your tongue, Colin Foster, or it's bed, broken leg or not!'

I was right, nothing has changed.

Well, they didn't redecorate my bedroom. Good thing too! They would have thrown away my posters or at least ripped them when they took them down. It's good to be back in here with my own books and things around me. That's one thing I'm glad hasn't changed. I wonder if I'll get a good night's sleep now I'm home again.

Tube in my arm,
Stuck in bed – boring.
Night on the farm,
Same old goat snoring.

What if I die
Just go away
Try not to cry
Not you mum, stay.

Straining to win,
Got to run faster.
Head in a spin
Scribbling on plaster.

Heartbeat is racing,
Scared of my dream.
Steady – just pacing,
Now there's that scream!
Scared by that sound;
'Don't let him kick me!'
Falls to the ground;
'Rob me and leave me!'

Stuck to the spot,
He's taken her purse now.
Stop him or not?
Wouldn't know how!

Pain in my head,
Rage of the witness.
Wish I were dead.
Frightened and helpless.

Must leave this place
Turn in disgrace
Race into space.
I knew that face . . .

WARREN